THREE STORIES includes 'He and His Man', written as Coetzee's acceptance speech for the Nobel Prize for Literature, 'A House in Spain' and 'Nietverloren'. This is their first appearance as a collection.

J. M. COETZEE was awarded the Nobel Prize for Literature in 2003 and was the first author to win the Booker Prize twice. His work includes *Waiting for the Barbarians*, *Life & Times of Michael K*, *The Master of Petersburg*, *Disgrace*, *Diary of a Bad Year* and *The Childhood of Jesus*. He lives in Adelaide.

THREE STORIES

THREE STORIES
J. M. COETZEE

TEXT PUBLISHING
MELBOURNE AUSTRALIA

The Text Publishing Company
22 William Street
Melbourne Victoria 3000
Australia
textpublishing.com.au

First published in this edition in Australia by
The Text Publishing Company, 2014.

'A House in Spain' first published in
Architectural Digest 57/10, 2000

'Nietverloren' first published as 'The African
Experience' in *Preservation* 54/2, 2002

'He and His Man' delivered as the Nobel Lecture, 2003

Book design by W. H. Chong
Printed and bound by Everbest Printing Co in China

National Library of Australia Cataloguing-in-Publication entry

Author: Coetzee, J. M., 1940– author.

Title: Three stories / by J. M. Coetzee.

ISBN: 9781922182562 (hardback)

ISBN: 9781925095500 (ebook)

Subjects: Short stories.

Dewey Number: A823.3

CONTENTS

A HOUSE IN SPAIN
(2000)

NIETVERLOREN
(2002)

HE AND HIS MAN
(2003)

I

A HOUSE IN SPAIN

AS HE GETS OLDER he finds himself growing more and more crabby about language, about slack usage, falling standards. Falling in love, for instance. "We fell in love with the house," friends of his say. How can you fall in love with a house when the house cannot love you back, he wants to reply? Once you start falling in love with objects, what will be left of real love, love as it used to be? But no one seems to care. People fall in love with tapestries, with old cars.

He would like to dismiss it, this neologism, this novelty, but he cannot. What if something is being revealed to him, some shift in the way people feel? What if the soul, which he had thought was made of timeless substance, is not timeless after all, but is in the process of growing lighter, less serious, accommodating itself to the times? What if falling in love with objects is no oddity any longer, for the soul—child's play, in fact? What if people around him do indeed feel, with the aid of their new, updated souls, in respect of real estate, the ache that he associates with falling in love? What, furthermore, if his own crabbiness expresses not what he tells himself it does—an old-fashioned fastidiousness about language—but on the contrary (he looks the idea squarely in the face) envy, the envy of a man grown too old, too rigid, to ever fall in love again?

The story of his own involvements with fixed property is easily told. In his lifetime he has owned, serially, two houses and an apartment, plus, for a while, in parallel, a seaside cottage. In all that history he can recollect nothing, by a long chalk, that he would grace with the name of love. In fact he can recollect little feeling at all, either when he took possession or when he moved out. Once he had put a house behind him he became quite incurious about its fate. More than incurious: he wanted never to see it again. Functional from beginning to end, his understanding of the ownership relation. Nothing like love, nothing like marriage.

He thinks about the women in his life, about his two marriages in particular. What does he still bear with him, within him, of those women, those wives? Tangles of emotion, for the most part: regret and sorrow pierced through with flashes of a feeling harder to pin down that may have something to do with shame but may equally have something to do with desire not yet dead.

Questions of love and ownership pre-occupy him, and there is a reason for that. A year ago he bought property abroad: in Spain, in Catalonia, on another continent. Property in Spain is not expensive, not off the coastline in Spain's decaying villages. Foreigners by the thousand, Europeans for the most part, but from elsewhere too, have acquired homes of a kind there, *pieds-à-terre*. Of whom he is now one.

In his case the move has its practical side. He makes his living as a writer; and in this day and age a writer can live anywhere, linked electronically to agents and editors as smoothly from a small village as from a city. Since his youth he has had a fondness for Spain, the Spain of taciturn pride and old formalities. (Does he love Spain? At least love of a country, a people, a way of life, is not some newfangled notion.) If he is going to spend more and more of his time in Spain, it makes sense to have a place he can call his own, a home where the linen and the kitchenware are familiar and he doesn't have to clean up other people's messes.

Of course one does not need to own Spanish property to spend time in Spain. One can work perfectly well out of rented accommodation, even out of hotels. Hotels might seem the expensive option, but not when one has done the arithmetic, added up all the incidentals. Hotels (thoughts of love keep coming back) are like passing affairs. One departs, parts company, and that is the end of it.

Buying a house may not make economic sense, but it makes a deeper kind of sense. He is in his fifties: if not in the final straight, then coming around the turn leading into the final straight. No more time for playing around, for following whims. The house in Catalonia is no impulse of the moment, no casual fling. On the contrary, it is the consequence of an eminently rational decision-making process. If it resembles a marriage at all, it resembles an arranged marriage, bridegroom matched with bride by a broker, a professional.

Yet even in arranged marriages man and wife sometimes fall in love. Is it possible that, late in life, he is going to fall in love with the house he has found for himself in Spain?

The house stands in a short street at the edge of the village of Bellpuig, overlooking fields of sunflower and corn. It comes with a huge fig tree and a patch of garden where he could, if he chose, grow his own beans and tomatoes. There is a rabbit hutch too, should his tastes incline to rabbit flesh. The house was built, if he is to believe the agent, in the thirteenth century. From the reading he has done on the antiquities of Catalonia, that is not impossible. The walls could certainly date back that far: they are a yard thick in places, meant to keep the cold of winter and the heat of summer out, the chiselled stone held together by crumbling mortar that by now might as well be sand.

In its structure the house will always be odd. The front double door opens on to a space so cavernous that it is fit to be used only as a garage and workshop, or else as an artist's studio. Up one side a staircase leads, via a hatch, to the living quarters and kitchen. The design makes sense only when one recognises that the core of the house used to be a barn, that the living space was constructed above and around the stabling so that human beings and cattle could share their blood warmth on the cold upland nights.

At the back the house is built into the side of a hill; a drain runs under the floor to bear rainwater away. As for the roof, the tiles are modern, with the stamp of a brickworks in Cervera; but the timbers are so worm-riddled, so powdery with rot, that they might well be centuries old too. Another few decades and the whole roof will probably come crashing down. But by then he will be beyond caring.

The previous owner (*the previous husband*, as he thinks of him) was a builder from Sant Climens, thirty kilometres away. It was he who fixed up the house, in his spare time, enlarging the windows, plastering the walls, replacing the doorframes, putting in new wiring, installing a bath and bidet, before selling it at a markup. No doubt he has moved on to another house now, some other project in some other village.

The locals have not been welcoming. The Spanish he speaks is of a hesitant, bookish variety that gets him nowhere in rural Catalonia, where Castilian is a foreign tongue. He is branded an outsider as soon as he opens his mouth. That is all right. He has no right to expect a welcome. What he hopes for, and what he gets, is toleration. Even in small villages, by now, people are used to outsiders moving in. Foreigners have been buying property in France, in Spain, in Portugal for years. The Spanish authorities have nothing against it. As long as they do not take jobs, as long as they bring in money, there is a place for foreigners.

It is the same in his own country, where the best seaside properties have passed into the hands of strangers. He does not necessarily like these strangers, with their bird-of-passage habits, but what do his likes and dislikes matter? His Catalan neighbours, he presumes, feel much the same about him: they do not necessarily like him; among themselves they probably complain about him and his kind; shopkeepers cheat him when they can, justifying themselves on the grounds that foreigners have too much money and are stupid anyway. But as to actively plotting harm against him, he doubts they would go that far. They will merely do nothing to make him feel at home, just as, when he is at home, he does nothing to make the Germans or the English feel at home.

During his first months in residence he spent hours every day working on the exterior.

———

He took down the front door, scraped it, painted it, rehung it. He did the same with the wooden shutters. Though his taste was for other colours, a whole other palette, he followed the colour scheme uniform to the village: a pale grey-blue; a deep red, here called Basque.

He took the door lock to pieces. The mechanism itself was primitive to the point of being laughable. A child could have picked it. Nevertheless he did not replace it, merely cleaned it, greased it, put it back. In this world, he told himself, locks are symbolic. A lock is here to make a statement about ownership, not to prevent a break-in, should anyone be so antisocial as to wish to break in.

He has bought the house, the house belongs to him, but only in a certain sense. In another sense it still belongs to the village in which it is embedded. Well, he has no ambition to prise the house loose from the village. He does not want it to be anything but what it is.

His plan, at the beginning, was to spend two seasons of the year here. Summers he would avoid because they were too hot, winters because they were too cold. Plenty of men have marriages like that, he told himself. Sailors, for instance, spend half their lives at sea.

But as the months passed he found something happening to him. He could not put the house from his mind. He lay awake at night, five thousand miles away, floating from room to room across the dark and empty interior. It was as though he were sending his soul across the seas, across the mountains, to the village wrapped in sleep: sending it or being called. Even in the daytime he had visions of involuntary, startling clarity: the rusty horseshoe nailed over the back door; the mould under the pipes in the bathroom; the stain, high up on the living-room wall, where a spider was crushed by a broom blow. There were moments when he was convinced that only by the force of his concentrated attention was the house being saved from inexistence.

So here he is, in midsummer, in Catalonia. In the cool of the morning he climbs on to the roof. On hands and knees, with a trowel, he begins to scratch away the moss that has grown between the tiles. From her balcony two doors down the street an old woman in black watches him. He hopes she approves. *A foreigner but a serious man*: that is what he hopes she thinks.

He grows geraniums, pink and red, in terracotta pots, and places them on either side of the front door, as the neighbours do. *Little attentions*, he calls them. Little attentions to the house, like the attentions one pays a woman.

If this is marriage, he tells himself, then it is a widow I am marrying, a mature woman, set in her ways. Just as I cannot be a different man, so I should not want her to become, for my sake, a different woman, younger, flashier, sexier.

By his labours he is, to some extent, breaking his unwritten compact with the village. When an outsider moves in and buys property, the compact says, he should bring profit to the local people: buy from the local merchants, give work to the local artisans. The work he is doing on the house belongs by right to those artisans. But on this point he will not yield. What he is engaged in is more serious than mere upkeep. It is intimate work, work he must do with his own hands. In time, he hopes, the local people will come to understand.

The village, of course, has memories of the house from before his time, and before the time of Sr Torras the jack-of-all-trades from Sant Climens. The villagers know—or if they do not know, then their parents and aunts and uncles knew—the family that used to live here, the family whose children grew up hating the dark, cramped rooms, the damp walls, the old-fashioned plumbing, and as soon as their parents died washed their hands of the place, selling it for a song to Sr Torras, who fixed it up and resold it to a foreigner because foreigners (inexplicably) prefer old houses and are prepared to pay more than they are worth to own them.

When one marries, one cares deeply who one's wife was married to before, even who she slept with before. With a house, one is not supposed to care who preceded one. That is another of the ways in which the analogy between ownership and marriage, houses and wives, is supposed to break down. But not in this case. Between these walls men and women, generation after generation, lived their intimate lives, talking and quarrelling and making love in a language he barely understands, according to habits that are foreign to him. They have left no ghosts behind, none that he can sense. But that does not matter. He broods on them, insofar as one can brood on people one has never so much as glimpsed. If he had photographs of them he would hang them on the walls: dour couples in their dark Sunday best, with their children crouching at their feet, humble as rabbits.

Why? Why does he want to remember people he never knew? For a good reason. When his own time here has passed, he does not want to be utterly forgotten. If the village will not remember him (he will die far away;

after a decent interval there will appear, without explanation, a new owner, a new face, and that will be that), then he hopes (hoping against hope) that in some sense the house itself will bear the memory of him.

What it comes down to, astonishingly, is that he wants a relationship with this house in a foreign country, a human relationship, however absurd the idea of a human relationship with stone and mortar might be. For the sake of that relationship, with this house and its history and the village as a whole, a village that, from the highway, looks as though it had been conceived by a single mind and built by a single pair of hands – in return for that relationship he is prepared to treat the house as one treats a woman, paying attention to her needs and even her quirks, spending money on her, soothing her through her bad times, treating her with kindness.

Kindness. Fidelity. Devotion. Service. Not love, not yet, but something like it. A form of marriage between a man growing old and a house no longer young.

NIETVERLOREN

FOR AS LONG AS HE could remember, from when he was first allowed to roam by himself out in the veld, out of sight of the farmhouse, he was puzzled by it: a circle of bare, flat earth ten paces across, its periphery marked with stones, a circle in which nothing grew, not a blade of grass.

He thought of it as a fairy circle, a circle

where fairies came at night to dance by the light of the tiny sparkling rods that they carried in the picturebooks he read, or perhaps by the light of glowworms. But in the picturebooks the fairy circle was always in a clearing in a forest, or else in a glen, whatever that might be. There were no forests in the Karoo, no glens, no glowworms; were there even fairies? What would fairies do with themselves in the daytime, in the stunned heat of summer, when it was too hot to dance, when even the lizards took shelter under stones? Would the fairies have enough sense to hide under stones too, or would they lie panting among the thornbushes, longing for England?

He asked his mother about the circle. Is it a fairy circle, he demanded? It can only be a fairy circle, she replied. He was not convinced.

They were visitors on the farm, though not particularly welcome visitors. They visited because they were family, and family were always entitled to visit. This particular visit had stretched on month after month: his father was away in the war, fighting the Italians, and they had nowhere else to go. He could have asked his grandmother what the circle was, but his grandmother never went into the veld, saw no sense in walking for the sake of walking. She would never have laid eyes on the circle, it was not the kind of thing that interested her.

The war ended; his father returned with a stiff little military moustache and a dapper, upright stride. They were back on the farm; he was walking with him in the veld. When they came to the circle, which he no longer called a fairy circle since he no longer believed in fairies, his father casually remarked, "Do you see that? That's the old threshing floor. That's where they used to thresh, in the old days."

Thresh: not a word he knew, but whatever

it meant, he did not like it. Too much like *thrash*. *Get a thrashing*: that was what happened to boys when they were naughty. *Naughty* was another word he drew back from. He did not want to be around when words like that were spoken.

Threshing turned out to be something one did with flails. There was a picture of it in the encyclopedia: men in funny old-fashioned clothes beating the ground with sticks with what look like bladders tied to them.

"But what are they *doing*?" he asked his mother.

"They are flailing the wheat," she replied."

"What is flailing?"

"Flailing is threshing. Flailing is beating."

"But *why*?"

"To separate the kernels of wheat from the chaff," she explained.

Flailing the wheat: it was all beyond him. Was he being asked to believe that once upon a time men used to beat wheat with bladders out in the veld? What wheat? Where did they get wheat to beat?

He asked his father. His father was vague. The threshing happened when he was small, he said; he was not paying attention. He was small, then he went away to boarding school; when he came back they were no longer threshing, perhaps because the drought killed the wheat, the drought of 1929 and 1930 and 1931, on and on, year after year.

That was the best his father could offer: not a fairy circle but a threshing floor, until the great drought came; then just a patch of earth where nothing grew. There the story rested for thirty years. After thirty years, back on the farm on what turned out to be his final visit, the story came up again, or if not the story in full then enough of it for him to be able to fill in the gaps. He was paging through photographs from the old days when he came upon a photograph of two young men with rifles, off on a hunt. In the background, not supposed to be part of the photograph, were two donkeys yoked together, and a man in tattered clothes, also not supposed to be in the picture, one hand on the yoke, squinting toward the camera from under his hat.

He peered more closely. Surely he recognised the site! Surely that was the threshing floor! The donkeys and their leader, captured in mid-stride sometime in the 1920s, were on the threshing floor, treading the wheat with their hooves, separating the grains from the chaff. If the photograph could come to life, if the two grinning young men were to pick up their rifles and disappear over the rim of the picture, he would at last have it before him, the whole mysterious business of threshing. The man with the hat, and the two donkeys, would resume their tread round and round the threshing floor, a tread that would, over the years, compact the earth so tightly that nothing would ever grow there. They would trample the wheat, and the wind—the wind that always blows in the Karoo, from horizon to horizon—would lift the chaff and whirl it away; the grain that was left behind would be gathered up and picked clean of straw and pebbles and ground small, ground to the finest flour, so that bread could be baked in the huge old wood-burning oven that used to dominate the farm kitchen.

But where did the wheat come from that the donkeys so patiently trod, donkeys dead now these many years, their bones cast out and picked clean by ants?

The wheat, it turned out (this was the

outcome of a long investigation, and even then he could not be sure if what he heard was true), was grown right here, on the farm, on what in the old days must have been cultivated land but has now reverted to bare veld. An acre of land had been given over to the growing of wheat, just as there had been an acre given over to pumpkin and squash and watermelon and sweetcorn and beans. Every day, from a dam that was just a pile of stones now, farmhands used to irrigate the acres; when the kernels turned brown, they reaped the wheat by hand, with sickles, bound it in sheaves, carted it to the threshing-floor, threshed it, then ground it to flour (he searched everywhere for the grinding stones, without success). From the bounty of those two acres the table was stocked not only of his grandfather but of all the families who worked for him. There were even cows kept, for milk, and pigs to eat the scraps.

So all those years ago this had been a self-sufficient farm, growing all its needs; and all the other farms in the neighbourhood, this vast, sparsely peopled neighbourhood, were self-sufficient too, more or less—farms where nothing grows any more, where no ploughing or sowing or tilling or reaping or threshing takes place, farms which have turned into vast grazing grounds for sheep, where farmers sit huddled over computers in darkened rooms calculating their profit and loss on sheepswool and lambsflesh.

Hunting and gathering, then pastoralism, then agriculture: those, he had been taught as a child, were the three stages in the ascent of man from savagery, an ascent whose end was not yet in sight. Who would have believed that there were places in the world where in the space of a century or two man would graduate from stage one to stage two to stage three and then regress to stage two. This Karoo, looked upon today as a desert on which flocks of ungulates barely clung to life, was not too long ago a region where hopeful farmers planted in the thin, rocky soil seeds brought from Europe and the New World, pumped water out of the artesian basin to keep them alive, subsisted on their fruits: a region of small, scattered peasant farmers and their labourers, independent, almost outside the money economy.

What put an end to it? No doubt the Great Drought disheartened many and drove them off the land. And no doubt, as the artesian basin was depleted over the years, they had to drill deeper and deeper for water. And of course who would want to break his back growing wheat and milling flour and baking bread when you had only to get in a car and drive for an hour to find a shop with racks and racks of ready-baked bread, to say nothing of pasteurised milk and frozen meat and vegetables?

Still, there was a larger picture. What did it mean for the land as a whole, and the conception the land had of itself, that huge tracts of it should be sliding back into prehistory? In the larger picture, was it really better that families who in the old days lived on the land by the sweat of their brow should now be mouldering in the windswept townships of Cape Town? Could one not imagine a different history and a different social order in which the Karoo was reclaimed, its scattered sons and daughters reassembled, the earth tilled again?

Bill and Jane, old friends from the United States, have arrived on a visit. Starting in the north of the country, they have driven in a hired car down the east coast; now the plan is that all four of them will drive from Cape Town to Johannesburg. The route, which runs for hundreds of miles through the Karoo, is not one that he likes. For reasons of his own he finds it depressing. But these are special friends, this is what they want to do, he does not demur.

"Didn't you say your grandfather had a farm in the Karoo?" says Bill. "Do we pass anywhere near there?"

"It's not in the family anymore," he replies. It is a lie. The farm is in the hands of his cousin Constant. Furthermore it does not take much of a detour off the Cape Town–Johannesburg road to get there. But he does not want to see the farm again, and what it has become, not in this life.

They leave Cape Town late in the day,

spend the first night in Matjiesfontein at the Lord Milner Hotel, where they are served dinner by waitresses in floral dresses and frilled Victorian caps. He and his wife sleep in the Olive Schreiner Room, their friends in the Baden Powell Room. On the walls of the Olive Schreiner room are watercolours of Karoo scenes ("Crossing the Drift", "Karoo Sunset"), photographs of cricketers: the Royal Fusiliers team of 1899, burly, moustachioed young Englishmen, come to die for their queen in a faroff land, some of them buried not far away.

The next morning they leave early. For hours they drive through empty scrubland ringed by flat-topped hills. Outside Richmond they stop for gas. Jane picks up a pamphlet. "NIETVERLOREN," it says. "Visit an old-style Karoo farm, experience old-style grace and simplicity. Only 15 km from Richmond on the Graaff–Reinet road. Luncheons 12–2."

They follow the signs to Nietverloren. At the turnoff a young man in a beret and khaki shirt scrambles to open the gate for them, stands to attention and salutes as they drive through.

The farmhouse, gabled in Cape Dutch style, brilliantly whitewashed, stands on an outcrop of rock overlooking fields and orchards. They are greeted at the door by a smiling young woman. "I'm Velma, I'm your hostess," she says, with a light, pleasing Afrikaans accent. They are the only guests thus far.

For lunch they are served leg of lamb and roast potatoes, braised baby carrots with raisins, roast pumpkin with cinnamon, followed by custard pie, *melktert*. "It's what we call *boerekos*," explains Velma, their hostess: "farm cuisine. Everything grown on the farm."

"And the bread?" he asks. "Do you grow your own wheat, and thresh it and all the rest?

Velma laughs lightly. "Good heavens no, we don't go as far back as that. But our bread is baked here in our kitchen, in our wood-fired oven, just like in the old days, as you will see on the tour."

They exchange glances. "I'm not sure we have time for a tour," he says. "How long does it take?"

"The tour is in two parts. First my husband takes you around the farm in the four-wheel drive. You see sheep-shearing, you see wool-sorting; if there are children they get to play with the lambs—the lambs are very cute. Then we've got a little museum, you can see all the grades of wool and the sheep-shearing instruments from the old days and the clothes people wore. Then I take you on a tour of the house, you see everything—the kitchen, which we have restored just as it used to be, and the bathroom, the old bathroom with the hip bath and the furnace, all just like in the old days, and everything else. Then you can relax, and at four o'clock we offer you tea."

"And how much is that?"

"For the tour and the tea together it is seventy-five rands per person."

He glances at Bill, at Jane. They are the guests, they must decide. Bill shakes his head. "It sounds fascinating, but I just don't think we have the time. Thank you, Velma."

They drive back through the orchard—grapevines, oranges, apricots heavy on the bough—past a pair of languid-eyed Jersey cows with calves by their side.

"Remarkable what they grow, considering how dry it is," says Jane.

"The soil is surprisingly fertile," he says.

"With enough water you could grow anything here. It could be a paradise."

"But—?"

"But it makes no economic sense. The only crop it makes sense to farm nowadays is people. The tourist crop. Places like Nietverloren are the only farms, if you can call them that, left in the Karoo: time-bubble, theme-park farms. The rest are just sheep ranches. There is no reason for the owners to live on them. They might as well be managed out of the cockpit of a helicopter. As in some cases they are. More enterprising landowners have gone back even further in time. They have got rid of the sheep and restocked their farms with game—antelope, zebra—and brought in hunters from overseas, from Germany and the US. A thousand rand for an eland, two thousand for a kudu. You shoot the animal, they mount the horns for you, you take them home with you on the plane. Trophies. The whole thing is called the safari experience, or sometimes just the African experience."

"You sound bitter."

"The bitterness of defeated love. I used to love this land. Then it fell into the hands of the entrepreneurs, and they gave it a makeover and a face-lift and put it on the market. This is the only future you have in South Africa, they told us: to be waiters and whores to the rest of the world. I want nothing to do with it."

A look passes between Bill and Jane. "I'm sorry," murmurs Jane.

Jane is sorry. He is sorry. All of them are a bit sorry, and not only for his outburst. Even Velma back on Nietverloren must be sorry for the charade she has to go through day after day, and the girls in their Victorian getup back in the hotel in Matjiesfontein: sorry and ashamed. A light grade of sorriness sits over the whole country, like cloud, like mist. But there is nothing to be done about it, nothing he can think of.

III

HE AND HIS MAN

BOSTON, ON THE COAST of Lincolnshire, is a handsome town, writes his man. The tallest church steeple in all of England is to be found there; sea-pilots use it to navigate by. Around Boston is fen country. Bitterns abound, ominous birds who give a heavy, groaning call loud enough to be heard two miles away, like the report of a gun.

The fens are home to many other kinds of birds too, writes his man, duck and mallard, teal and widgeon, to capture which the men of the fens, the fen-men, raise tame ducks, which they call decoy ducks or duckoys.

Fens are tracts of wetland. There are tracts of wetland all over Europe, all over the world, but they are not named fens, *fen* is an English word, it will not migrate.

These Lincolnshire duckoys, writes his man, are bred up in decoy ponds, and kept tame by being fed by hand. Then when the season comes they are sent abroad to Holland and Germany. In Holland and Germany they meet with others of their kind, and, seeing how miserably these Dutch and German ducks live, how their rivers freeze in winter and their lands are covered in snow, fail not to let them know, in a form of language which they make them understand, that in England

from where they come the case is quite other-
wise: English ducks have seashores full of
nourishing food, tides that flow freely up the
creeks; they have lakes, springs, open ponds
and sheltered ponds; also lands full of corn left
behind by the gleaners; and no frost or snow,
or very light.

By these representations, he writes,
which are made all in duck language, they, the
decoy ducks or duckoys, draw together vast
numbers of fowl and, so to say, kidnap them.
They guide them back across the seas from
Holland and Germany and settle them down
in their decoy ponds on the fens of Lincolnshire, chattering and gabbling to them all the
time in their own language, telling them these
are the ponds they told them of, where they
shall live safely and securely.

And while they are so occupied the
decoy men, the masters of the decoy ducks,

creep into covers or coverts they have built of reeds upon the fens, and all unseen toss handfuls of corn upon the water; and the decoy ducks or duckoys follow them, bringing their foreign guests behind. And so over two or three days they lead their guests up narrower and narrower waterways, calling to them all the time to see how well we live in England, to a place where nets have been spanned.

Then the decoy men send out their decoy dog, which has been perfectly trained to swim after fowl, barking as he swims. Being alarmed to the last degree by this terrible creature, the ducks take to the wing, but are forced down again into the water by the arched nets above, and so must swim or perish, under the net. But the net grows narrower and narrower, like a purse, and at the end stand the decoy men, who take their captives out one by one. The decoy ducks are stroked and made much of, but as for their guests, these are clubbed on the spot and plucked and sold by the hundred and by the thousand.

All of this news of Lincolnshire his man writes in a neat, quick hand, with quills that he sharpens with his little penknife each day before a new bout with the page.

In Halifax, writes his man, there stood, until it was removed in the reign of King James I, an engine of execution, which worked thus. The condemned man was laid with his head on the cross-base or cup of the scaffold; then the executioner knocked out a pin which held up the heavy blade. The blade descended down a frame as tall as a church door and beheaded the man as clean as a butcher's knife.

Custom had it in Halifax, though, that if between the knocking out of the pin and the descent of the blade the condemned man could leap to his feet, run down the hill, and swim across the river without being seized again by the executioner, he would be let free. But in all the years the engine stood in Halifax this never happened.

He (not his man now but he) sits in his room by the waterside in Bristol and reads this. He is getting on in years, almost it might be said he is an old man by now. The skin of his face, that had been almost blackened by the tropic sun before he made a parasol out of palm or palmetto leaves to shade himself, is paler now, but still leathery like parchment; on his nose is a sore from the sun that will not heal.

The parasol he has still with him in his room, standing in a corner, but the parrot that came back with him has passed away. *Poor Robin!* the parrot would squawk from its perch on his shoulder, *Poor Robin Crusoe! Who shall save poor Robin?* His wife could not abide the lamenting of the parrot, *Poor Robin* day in, day out. *I shall wring its neck*, said she, but she had not the courage to do so.

When he came back to England from his island with his parrot and his parasol and his chest full of treasure, he lived for a while tranquilly enough with his old wife on the estate he bought in Huntingdon, for he had become a wealthy man, and wealthier still after the printing of the book of his adventures. But the years on the island, and then the years travelling with his serving-man Friday (poor Friday, he laments to himself, squawk-squawk, for the parrot would never speak Friday's name, only his), had made the life of a landed gentleman dull for him. And, if the truth be told, married life was a sore disappointment too. He found himself retreating more and more to the stables, to his horses, which blessedly did not chatter, but whinnied softly when he came, to show that they knew who he was, and then held their peace.

It seemed to him, coming from his island, where until Friday arrived he lived a silent life, that there was too much speech in the world. In bed beside his wife he felt as if a shower of pebbles were being poured upon his head, in an unending rustle and clatter, when all he desired was to sleep.

So when his old wife gave up the ghost he mourned but was not sorry. He buried her and after a decent while took this room in the *Jolly Tar* on the Bristol waterfront, leaving the direction of the estate in Huntingdon to his son, bringing with him only the parasol from the island that made him famous and the dead parrot fixed to its perch and a few necessaries, and has lived here alone ever since, strolling by day about the wharves and quays, staring out west over the sea, for his sight is still keen, smoking his pipes. As to his meals, he has these brought up to his room; for he finds no joy in society, having grown used to solitude on the island.

He does not read, he has lost the taste for it; but the writing of his adventures has put him in the habit of writing, it is a pleasant enough recreation. In the evening by candle-light he will take out his papers and sharpen his quills and write a page or two of his man, the man who sends report of the duckoys of Lincolnshire, and of the great engine of death in Halifax, that one can escape if before the awful blade can descend one can leap to one's feet and dash down the hill, and of numbers of other things. Every place he goes he sends report of, that is his first business, this busy man of his.

Strolling along the harbour wall,

reflecting upon the engine from Halifax, he, Robin, whom the parrot used to call poor Robin, drops a pebble and listens. A second, less than a second, before it strikes the water. God's grace is swift, but might not the great blade of tempered steel, being heavier than a pebble and being greased with tallow, be swifter? How will we ever escape it? And what species of man can it be who will dash so busily hither and thither across the kingdom, from one spectacle of death to another (clubbings, beheadings), sending in report after report?

A man of business, he thinks to himself. Let him be a man of business, a grain merchant or a leather merchant, let us say; or a manufacturer and purveyor of roof tiles somewhere where clay is plentiful, Wapping let us say, who must travel much in the interest of his trade. Make him prosperous, give him a wife who loves him and does not chatter too much and bears him children, daughters mainly; give him a reasonable happiness; then bring his happiness suddenly to an end. The Thames rises one winter, the kilns in which the tiles are baked are washed away, or the grain stores, or the leather works; he is ruined, this man of his, debtors descend upon him like flies or like crows, he has to flee his home, his wife, his children, and seek hiding in the most wretched of quarters in Beggars Lane under a false name and in disguise. And all of this—the wave of water, the ruin, the flight, the pennilessness, the tatters, the solitude—let all of this be a figure of the shipwreck and the island where he, poor Robin, was secluded from the world for twenty-six years, till he almost went mad (and indeed, who is to say he did not, in some measure?).

Or else let the man be a saddler with a home and a shop and a warehouse in

Whitechapel and a mole on his chin and a wife who loves him and does not chatter and bears him children, daughters mainly, and gives him much happiness, until the plague descends upon the city, it is the year 1665, the great fire of London has not yet come. The plague descends upon London: daily, parish by parish, the count of the dead mounts, rich and poor, for the plague makes no distinction among stations, all this saddler's worldly wealth will not save him. He sends his wife and daughters into the countryside and makes plans to flee himself, but then does not. *Thou shalt not be afraid for the terror at night*, he reads, opening the Bible at hazard, *not for the arrow that flieth by day; not for the pestilence that walketh in darkness; nor for the destruction that wasteth at noonday. A thousand shall fall at thy side, and ten thousand at thy right hand, but it shall not come nigh thee.*

Taking heart from this sign, a sign of

safe passage, he remains in afflicted London and sets about writing reports. *I came upon a crowd in the street,* he writes, *and a woman in its midst pointing to the heavens. See,* she cries, *an angel in white brandishing a flaming sword! And all in the crowd nod among themselves. Indeed it is so,* they say: *an angel with a sword!* But he, the saddler, can see no angel, no sword. All he can see is a strange-shaped cloud brighter on the one side than the other, from the shining of the sun.

It is an allegory! cries the woman in the street; but he can see no allegory for the life of him. Thus in his report.

On another day, walking by the riverside in Wapping, his man that used to be a saddler but now has no occupation observes how a woman from the door of her house calls out to a man rowing in a dory: *Robert! Robert!* she calls; and how the man then rows ashore, and from the dory takes up a sack which he lays upon a stone by the riverside, and rows away again; and how the woman comes down to the riverside and picks up the sack and bears it home, very sorrowful looking.

He accosts the man Robert and speaks to him. Robert informs him that the woman is his wife and the sack holds a week's supplies for her and their children, meat and meal and butter; but that he dare not approach nearer, for all of them, wife and children, have the plague upon them; and that it breaks his heart. And all of this—the man Robert and wife keeping communion through calls across the water, the sack left by the waterside—stands for itself certainly, but stands also as a figure of his, Robinson's, solitude on his island, where in his hour of darkest despair he called out across the waves to his loved ones in England to save him, and at other times swam out to the wreck in search of supplies.

Further report from that time of woe. Able no longer to bear the pain from the swellings in the groin and armpit that are the signs of the plague, a man runs out howling, stark naked, into the street, into Harrow Alley in Whitechapel, where his man the saddler witnesses him as he leaps and prances and makes a thousand strange gestures, his wife and children running after him crying out, calling to him to come back. And this leaping and prancing is allegoric of his own leaping and prancing when, after the calamity of the shipwreck and after he had scoured the strand for sign of his shipboard companions and found none, save a pair of shoes that were not mates, he had understood he was cast up all alone on a savage island, likely to perish and with no hope of salvation.

(But of what else does he secretly sing, he wonders to himself, this poor afflicted man of whom he reads, besides his desolation? What is he calling, across the waters and across the years, out of his private fire?)

A year ago he, Robinson, paid two guineas to a sailor for a parrot the sailor had brought back from, he said, Brazil—a bird not so magnificent as his own well-beloved creature but splendid nonetheless, with green feathers and a scarlet crest and a great talker too, if the sailor was to be believed. And indeed the bird would sit on its perch in his room in the inn, with a little chain on its leg in case it should try to fly away, and say the words *Poor Poll! Poor Poll!* over and over till he was forced to hood it; but could not be taught to say any other word, *Poor Robin!* for instance, being perhaps too old for that.

Poor Poll, gazing out through the narrow

window over the mast-tops and, beyond the mast-tops, over the grey Atlantic swell: *What island is this*, asks Poor Poll, *that I am cast up on, so cold, so dreary? Where were you, my Saviour, in my hour of great need?*

A man, being drunk and it being late at night (another of his man's reports), falls asleep in a doorway in Cripplegate. The dead-cart comes on its way (we are still in the year of the plague), and the neighbours, thinking the man dead, place him on the dead-cart among the corpses. By and by the cart comes to the dead pit at Mountmill and the carter, his face all muffled against the effluvium, lays hold of him to throw him in; and he wakes up and struggles in his bewilderment. *Where am I?* he says. *You are about to be buried among the dead*, says the carter. *But am I dead then?* says the man. And this too is a figure of him on his island.

Some London folk continue to go about their business, thinking they are healthy and will be passed over. But secretly they have the plague in their blood: when the infection reaches the heart they fall dead upon the spot, so reports his man, as if struck by lightning. And this is a figure for life itself, the whole of life. Due preparation. We should make due preparation for death, or else be struck down where we stand. As he, Robinson, was made to see when of a sudden, on his island, he came one day upon the footprint of a man in the sand. It was a print, and therefore a sign: of a foot, of a man. But it was a sign of much else too. *You are not alone*, said the sign; and also, *No matter how far you sail, no matter where you hide, you will be searched out.*

In the year of the plague, writes his man, others, out of terror, abandoned all, their homes, their wives and children, and fled as far from London as they could. When the plague had passed, their flight was condemned as cowardice on all sides. But, writes his man, we forget what kind of courage was called on to confront the plague. It was not a mere soldier's courage, like gripping a weapon and charging the foe: it was like charging Death himself on his pale horse.

Even at his best, his island parrot, the better loved of the two, spoke no word he was not taught to speak by his master. How then has it come about that this man of his, who is a kind of parrot and not much loved, writes as well as or better than his master? For he wields an able pen, this man of his, no doubt of that. *Like charging Death himself on his pale horse.* His own skill, learned in the counting house, was in making tallies and accounts, not in turning phrases. *Death himself on his pale horse*: those are words he would not think of. Only when he yields himself up to this man of his do such words come.

And decoy ducks, or duckoys: What did he, Robinson, know of decoy ducks? Nothing at all, until this man of his began sending in reports.

The duckoys of the Lincolnshire fens, the great engine of execution in Halifax: reports from a great tour this man of his seems to be making of the island of Britain, which is a figure of the tour he made of his own island in the skiff he built, the tour that showed there was a farther side to the island, craggy and dark and inhospitable, which he ever afterwards avoided, though if in the future colonists shall arrive upon the island they will perhaps explore it and settle it; that too being a figure, of the dark side of the soul and the light.

When the first bands of plagiarists and imitators descended upon his island history and foisted on the public their own feigned stories of the castaway life, they seemed to him no more or less than a horde of cannibals falling upon his own flesh, that is to say, his life; and he did not scruple to say so. *When I defended myself against the cannibals, who sought to strike me down and roast me and devour me*, he wrote, *I thought I defended myself against the thing itself. Little did I guess*, he wrote, *that these cannibals were but figures of a more devilish voracity, that would gnaw at the very substance of truth.*

But now, reflecting further, there begins to creep into his breast a touch of fellow feeling for his imitators. For it seems to him now that there are but a handful of stories in the world; and if the young are to be forbidden to prey upon the old then they must sit for ever in silence.

Thus in the narrative of his island adventures he tells of how he awoke in terror one night convinced the devil lay upon him in his bed in the shape of a huge dog. So he leapt to his feet and grasped a cutlass and slashed left and right to defend himself while the poor parrot that slept by his bedside shrieked in alarm. Only many days later did he understand that neither dog nor devil had lain upon him, but rather that he had suffered a palsy of a passing kind, and being unable to move his leg had concluded there was some creature stretched out upon it. Of which event the lesson would seem to be that all afflictions, including the palsy, come from the devil and are the very devil; that a visitation by illness may be figured as a visitation by the devil, or by a dog figuring the devil, and vice versa, the visitation figured as an illness, as in the saddler's history of the plague; and therefore that no one who writes stories of either, the devil or the plague, should forthwith be dismissed as a forger or a thief.

When, years ago, he resolved to set down on paper the story of his island, he found that the words would not come, the pen would not flow, his very fingers were stiff and reluctant. But day by day, step by step, he mastered the writing business, until by the time of his adventures with Friday in the frozen north the pages were rolling off easily, even thoughtlessly.

That old ease of composition has, alas, deserted him. When he seats himself at the little writing-desk before the window looking over Bristol harbour, his hand feels as clumsy and the pen as foreign an instrument as ever before.

Does he, the other one, that man of his,

find the writing business easier? The stories he writes of ducks and machines of death and London under the plague flow prettily enough; but then so did his own stories once. Perhaps he misjudges him, that dapper little man with the quick step and the mole upon his chin. Perhaps at this very moment he sits alone in a hired room somewhere in this wide kingdom dipping the pen and dipping it again, full of doubts and hesitations and second thoughts.

How are they to be figured, this man and he? As master and slave? As brothers, twin brothers? As comrades in arms? Or as enemies, foes? What name shall he give this nameless fellow with whom he shares his evenings and sometimes his nights too, who is absent only in the daytime, when he, Robin, walks the quays inspecting the new arrivals and his man gallops about the kingdom making his inspections?

Will this man, in the course of his travels, ever come to Bristol? He yearns to meet the fellow in the flesh, shake his hand, take a stroll with him along the quayside and hearken as he tells of his visit to the dark north of the island, or of his adventures in the writing business. But he fears there will be no meeting, not in this life. If he must settle on a likeness for the pair of them, his man and he, he would write that they are like two ships sailing in contrary directions, one west, the other east. Or better, that they are deckhands toiling in the rigging, the one on a ship sailing west, the other on a ship sailing east. Their ships pass close, close enough to hail. But the seas are rough, the weather is stormy: their eyes lashed by the spray, their hands burned by the cordage, they pass each other by, too busy even to wave.